Two boys imaginatively explore the moon from high in a tree on a summer night.

Skip
Aboard
a
Space Ship

By Jane Belk Moncure

Illustrated by
Helen Endres

THE
CHILD'S
WORLD
ELGIN, ILLINOIS 60120

Library of Congress Cataloging in Publication Data

Moncure, Jane Belk.
  Skip aboard a space ship.

  (Creative dramatics)
  SUMMARY: Two boys spending the night in a tree
house pretend they are taking a trip to the moon.
  [1. Space flight to the moon—Fiction. 2. Play—
Fiction] I. Endres, Helen. II. Title. III. Series.
PZ7.M739Sk   [E]   77-12958
ISBN 0-89565-009-6

Distributed by Childrens Press, 1224 West Van Buren Street, Chicago, Illinois 60607.

Skip
Aboard
a
Space Ship

This was a very special night. Dad had promised Skip that he and Eric could sleep in the tree house.

As they scrambled into their sleeping bags, Skip said, "Look at that moon! Wow! It will be our light all night!"

It was late, but Skip did not close his eyes.
"Eric," he said, "just think! The astronauts
went to that moon in a moon rocket."

"I can almost see a rocket out there," said Eric. "You know what? This place could be a space ship. Let's go to the moon tonight!"

"Good idea!"

"Zip up your space suit," called Eric. "Put on your space helmet."

"Count down. . .
five,
   four,
      three,
         two,
            one,
               zero!
Lift off!''

"We're flying through space!''

"Zoom!" said Skip. "There goes the first stage booster rocket."

"Zoom! There goes the second."

"We are way up in the command module. You and I are co-pilots."

"Earth is far away now," said Eric. "It is getting smaller and smaller."

"We're right on course! Fire the third stage booster rocket."

"Fire!"

"Let's talk to ground control. Hey, Dad!"
Skip's Dad flashed on his flashlight. "Are
you two boys O.K.?" he called.

"Sure! We're on a mission to the moon!"

"Watch out for those deep craters," said
Dad. "Find a soft spot to land. I'm going to
bed."

"I see a deep crater!" said Eric. "Watch out! Get into the lunar landing module."

"Slow down!"

"We are about to land!"

"We made it!" Skip breathed a great, deep sigh.

"Put on your moon suit," commanded Eric. "Don't forget your oxygen supply. There isn't any air up here."

"Wow!" called Skip. "I can jump twenty feet high! It's like flying!"

"Let's climb a moon mountain," said Eric. "Don't fall."

19

"Here's the old lunar rover the astronauts left up here," said Skip. "Let's take a ride."

"Stop the rover!" Eric called. "I'm going to collect some moon rocks."

"You will be a famous astronaut," said Skip. "Your rocks will be in museums all around the world."

"I know."

Soon Skip said, "My oxygen supply is low. Quick, let's get back to the lunar landing module and fire up the rockets."

"Up and away!"

"Good-by moon!"

"We are docking with our space ship," said
Skip. "What a trip!"
"I'm tired," said Eric.

"Don't go to sleep," shouted Skip. "There's the new space station above the earth. Let's stop there and take the new space shuttle back to earth."

"No," said Eric. "Let's splash down in the ocean! That would be more fun."

"O.K."

"Wow!" said Skip. "We are blazing like a ball of fire! The parachutes are unfolding! Get ready for the splash down!"

"We made it!" said Skip.

Eric did not answer. He was already asleep.

Creative dramatics provides a framework for the expression of many emotions and thoughts. Children are constantly dramatizing events that have happened to them, characters and situations they have seen on television, and happenings people have discussed with them. Through imaginative play, a child restructures his own experiences and discovers new ones. By imitating others in play, he comes to understand what they do and why, and also how their actions affect him.

About the Author:

Jane Belk Moncure, author of many books and stories for young children, is a graduate of Virginia Commonwealth University and Columbia University. She has taught nursery, kindergarten and primary children in Europe and America. Mrs. Moncure has taught early childhood education while serving on the faculties of Virginia Commonwealth University and the University of Richmond. She was the first president of the Virginia Association for Early Childhood Education and has been recognized widely for her services to young children. She is married to Dr. James A. Moncure, Vice President of Elon College, and currently lives in Burlington, North Carolina.

About the Artist:

Helen Endres is a commercial artist, designer and illustrator of children's books. She has lived and worked in the Chicago area since coming from her native Oklahoma in 1952. Graduated from Tulsa University with a BA, she received further training at Hallmark in Kansas City and from the Chicago Art Institute. Ms. Endres attributes much of her creative achievement to the advice and encouragement of her Chicago contemporaries and to the good humor and patience of the hundreds of young models who have posed for her.